D1381838

Editor - Zachary Rau
Contributing Editors - Robert Buscemi
Graphic Designer and Letterer - John Lo and Louis Csontos
Cover Designer - Gary Shum

Digital Imaging Manager - Chris Buford
Production Managers - Jennifer Miller and Mutsumi Miyazaki
Senior Designer - Anna Kernbaum
Senior Editor - Elizabeth Hurchalla
Managing Editor - Lindsey Johnston
VP of Production - Ron Klamert
Publisher & Editor in Chief - Mike Kiley
President & C.O.O. - John Parker
C.E.O. - Stuart Levy

E-mail: info@TOKYOPOP.com
Come visit us online at www.TOKYOPOP.com
Visit the official Star Wars website at www.starwars.com

A **TOKYOPOP** Cine-Manga® Book
TOKYOPOP Inc.
5900 Wilshire Blvd., Suite 2000
Los Angeles, CA 90036

Star Wars: Revenge of the Sith

ISBN: 1-59532-977-3

First TOKYOPOP® printing: November 2005

10 9 8 7 6 5 4 3 2 1

Printed in Italy

STAR WARS

EPISODE III
REVENGE OF
THE SITH

STORY AND SCREENPLAY BY
GEORGE LUCAS

HAMBURG • LONDON • LOS ANGELES • TOKYO

PADMÉ AMIDALA:
BELOVED SENATOR
FROM NABOO

ANAKIN SKYWALKER:
A YOUNG JEDI OF
EXTRAORDINARY PROMISE

OBI-WAN KENOBI:
ANAKIN'S JEDI MENTOR
AND BEST FRIEND

YODA:
A JEDI MASTER OF
SINGULAR POWER, REVERED
FOR HIS WISDOM

DARTH SIDIOUS:
LORD OF THE SITH

MACE WINDU:
A JEDI MASTER WHO SITS
ON THE JEDI COUNCIL

CHANCELLOR PALPATINE:
HEAD OF THE GALACTIC
REPUBLIC ON CORUSCANT

SENATOR BAIL ORGANA:
A VIRTUOUS STATESMAN
FROM ALDERAAN

GENERAL GRIEVOUS:
SUPREME COMMANDER OF THE
DROID ARMIES—RUTHLESS
AND POWERFUL

A long time ago in a galaxy far, far away....

War! The Republic is crumbling under attacks by the ruthless Sith Lord, Count Dooku. There are heroes on both sides. Evil is everywhere.

In a stunning move, the fiendish droid leader, General Grievous, has swept into the Republic capital and kidnapped Chancellor Palpatine, leader of the Galactic Senate.

As the Separatist Droid Army attempts to flee the besieged capital with their valuable hostage, two Jedi Knights lead a desperate mission to rescue the captive Chancellor....

ANAKIN LINES UP AND FIRES, TAKING OUT A FEW BUZZ DROIDS, BUT ALSO CAUSING FURTHER DAMAGE TO OBI-WAN'S SHIP.

In the name of--!! Hold your fire! You're not helping here!

I agree. Bad idea.

I can't see a thing! My cockpit's fogging! They're all over me, Anakin!

Move to the right.

AS THE BATTLE INTENSIFIES, COUNT DOOKU FORCE-CHOKES OBI-WAN...

...THROWING HIM INTO A WALL, KNOCKING HIM OUT...

...AND COLLAPSING THE WALKWAY ABOVE ON TOP OF HIM.

ANAKIN MUST FIGHT DOOKU ALONE...AGAIN.

I sense great fear in you, Skywalker. You have hate, you have anger, but you don't use them.

INFURIATED BY DOOKU'S COMMENTS, ANAKIN ATTACKS THE SITH LORD WITH LIGHTNING SPEED...

...AND SEVERS BOTH COUNT DOOKU'S HANDS.

16

Wait...! Obi-Wan!

Anakin, there is no time. We must get off the ship before it's too late.

He seems to be all right.

Leave him, or we'll never make it!

His fate will be the same as ours.

ON THE BRIDGE, GENERAL GRIEVOUS PREPARES TO ENGAGE THE REPUBLIC FLEET.

PREPARE FOR ATTACK! ALL BATTERIES FIRE! FIRE!

TURBOLASER FIRE RUPTURES THE SHIP'S HULL...

Today, you are the hero and you deserve your glorious day with the politicians.

All right, but you owe me. And not for saving your skin for the tenth time...

Chancellor Palpatine, are you all right?

Yes, thanks to your two Jedi Knights. They killed Count Dooku, but General Grievous has escaped once again.

General Grievous will run and hide as he always does. He is a coward!

But with Count Dooku dead, he is the leader of the Droid Army, and I assure you, the Senate will vote to continue the war as long as Grievous is alive.

Then the Jedi Council will make finding Grievous our highest priority.

LATER, IN PALPATINE'S OFFICE...

Anakin, I'm appointing you to be my personal representative on the Jedi Council.

Me? A Master? I am overwhelmed, sir. The Council elects its own members. They will never accept this.

AND SO, THE JEDI COUNCIL DELIBERATES ON THEIR NEW APPOINTMENT.

I think they will. They need you more than you know.

Allow this appointment lightly, the Council does not. Disturbing, is this move by Chancellor Palpatine.

You are on this Council, but we do not grant you the rank of Master.

What?! How can you be on the Council and not be a Master?!

Take a seat, young Skywalker.

Hiding in the Outer Rim, Grievous is. The outlying systems, you must sweep.

What about the droid attack on the Wookiees?

Go, I will. Good relations with the Wookiees, I have.

It is settled then. Yoda will take a battalion of clones to reinforce the Wookiees on Kashyyyk. May the Force be with us all.

ANAKIN FUMES AS THE COUNCIL ADJOURNS...

What kind of nonsense is this?! They put me on the Council and don't make me a Master?! It's insulting!

Calm down, Anakin! You have been given a great honor. To be on the Council at your age--it's never happened before.

The fact of the matter is, the Council doesn't like it when the Chancellor interferes in Jedi affairs.

I swear to you, I didn't ask to be put on the Council...

But that's what you wanted!

Your friendship with Chancellor Palpatine seems to have paid off.

That has nothing to do with this.

The only reason the Council has approved your appointment is because the Chancellor trusts you.

The Council wants you to report on all of the Chancellor's dealings. They want to know what he's up to.

They want me to spy on the Chancellor? That's treason!

We are at war, Anakin.

Why didn't the Council give me this assignment when we were in session?

This assignment is not to be on record.

That is why you must help us, Anakin. Our allegiance is to the Senate, not to its leader, who has managed to stay in office long after his term has expired.

You're asking me to do something against the Jedi Code. Against the Republic. Against a mentor...and a friend. That's what's out of place here. Why are you asking this of me?

The Council is asking you.

Tell your people to take shelter. If you have warriors, now is the time.

Arfour, take the fighter back to the ship. Tell Commander Cody I've made contact.

BEEP-BOOP MEEP.

TO FACILITATE THE HUNT FOR GENERAL GRIEVOUS OVER UTAPAU'S TREACHEROUS LANDSCAPE...

...OBI-WAN HOPS ABOARD THE INDIGENOUS TRANSPORTATION, THE AMAZING LIZARD BOGA.

INSIDE ONE OF THE PLANET'S SINKHOLES, OBI-WAN SEARCHES FOR GENERAL GRIEVOUS...

ONLY TO FINALLY FIND HIM AND THE COUNCIL OF SEPARATISTS HIDING IN A DESERTED HANGAR.

It won't be long before the armies of the Republic track us here.

I am sending you all to the Mustafar system in the Outer Rim.

OBI-WAN HIDES IN THE SHADOWS, LISTENING TO THE SECRET MEETING.

It is a volcanic planet which generates a great deal of scanning interference. You will be safe there.

Safe?! Chancellor Palpatine managed to escape your grip, General. I have doubts about your ability to keep us safe.

Be thankful, Viceroy, that you have not found yourself in my grip. Your ship is waiting.

JUST THEN, OBI-WAN REVEALS HIMSELF.

Hello there!

General Kenobi!

You are a bold one.

Your move.

ANAKIN RELAYS THE MESSAGE TO THE CHANCELLOR.

Chancellor, we have just received a report from Master Kenobi. He has engaged General Grievous.

We can only hope that Master Kenobi is up to the challenge.

It is upsetting to me to see that the Council doesn't seem to fully appreciate your talents.

Don't you wonder why they won't make you a Jedi Master?

They know your power will be too strong to control. You must break through the fog of lies the Jedi have created around you. Let me help you to know the subtleties of the Force.

How do you know the ways of the Force?

My mentor taught me everything about the Force...even the nature of the dark side.

MEANWHILE, OBI-WAN CONTINUES HIS PURSUIT OF GENERAL GRIEVOUS.

GRIEVOUS STEERS THE CHASE ONTO A SECRET LANDING PLATFORM...

...GRABS A HIDDEN BLASTER AND FIRES, TRYING TO FINISH THE JEDI OFF.

OBI-WAN PRIES THE GUN FROM GRIEVOUS, BUT IS KNOCKED DOWN IN THE PROCESS...

...AND GRIEVOUS POUNCES ON THE JEDI, KNOCKING HIM OFF THE EDGE OF THE LANDING PLATFORM.

When the Jedi learn what has transpired here, they will kill us along with all the Senators.

I agree. The Jedi's next move will be against the Senate.

Every single Jedi, including your friend Obi-Wan Kenobi, is now an enemy of the Republic.

I understand, Master.

First, I want you to go to the Jedi Temple. Do what must be done, Lord Vader. Do not hesitate. Show no mercy.

Only then will you be strong enough with the dark side to save Padmé.

What about the other Jedi spread across the galaxy?

Their betrayal will be dealt with. After you have killed all the Jedi in the Temple, go to the Mustafar system.

ACROSS THE GALAXY ON UTAPAU, THE BATTLE BETWEEN THE CLONES AND THE DROIDS RAGES ON...

Commander Cody, contact your troops. Tell them to move to the higher levels.

Very good, sir.

OBI-WAN RIDES THE GIGANTIC LIZARD BACK INTO BATTLE...

...AS DARTH SIDIOUS PUTS ANCIENT PLANS INTO ACTION.

It will be done, My Lord.

Commander Cody, the time has come. Execute Order 66!

Blast him!

COMMANDER CODY ORDERS HIS CLONE TROOPERS TO ATTACK OBI-WAN, KNOCKING HIM OFF THE BOGA AND SENDING HIM PLUMMETING DOWN A HUNDRED-FOOT SINKHOLE.

ON UTAPAU, OBI-WAN CRAWLS TO SHORE...

...BOARDS GENERAL GRIEVOUS' STARFIGHTER...

...AND DESPERATELY ATTEMPTS TO SEND A DISTRESS SIGNAL.

Emergency Code 913. I have no contact on any frequency!

Zzzzt...Kenobi... Ksssshhht!

Repeat!

Master Kenobi?!

Senator Organa! My Clone Troops turned on me! I need help!

We have just rescued Master Yoda. It appears this ambush has happened everywhere. We're sending you our coordinates!

BACK ON MUSTAFAR, ANAKIN MAKES SHORT WORK OF NUTE GUNRAY AND THE SEPARATIST LEADERS...

...DISMANTLING PALPATINE'S CIRCLE OF POWER IN A FLASH.

ON CORUSCANT, THE SENATE CONTINUES TO MEET...

The attempt on my life has left me scarred and deformed, but I must assure you my resolve has never been stronger.

In order to ensure our security and continuing stability, the Republic will be reorganized into the first Galactic Empire for a safe and secure society!

So this is how liberty dies, with thunderous applause.

You will not stop me. Darth Vader will become more powerful than either of us.

Not if anything, I have to say about it. At an end, your rule is.

ELSEWHERE, THE BATTLE BETWEEN YODA AND DARTH SIDIOUS SPILLS OUT INTO THE SENATE CHAMBERS.

PALPATINE FORCE-THROWS A FLOATING PLATFORM AT YODA...

...BUT AS YODA JUMPS OUT OF THE WAY...

...HE IS STRUCK BY FORCE-LIGHTING IN MID-AIR.

YODA BARELY GRABS ONTO A PLATFORM...

...BUT HIS GRIP FAILS HIM...

...AND HE PLUMMETS HUNDREDS OF METERS DOWN TO THE FLOOR OF THE SENATE CHAMBERS.

DAZED AND EXHAUSTED, YODA REALIZES HE HAS UNDERESTIMATED THE DARK LORD AND CALLS BAIL ORGANA FOR HELP.

Hurry. Careful timing we will need.

YODA IS RESCUED BY BAIL AND ESCAPES, NEVER TO RETURN TO CORUSCANT.

Into exile, I must go.

Failed, I have...

MEMBERS OF THE
JEDI ORDER

KI–ADI–MUNDI

- Homeworld: Cerea
- Species: Cerean
- Gender: Male
- Height: 1.98 meters

Along with Mace Windu and Yoda, Ki-Adi-Mundi was a member of the upper tier of the Council. His most distinguishing physical feature was an enlarged conical cranium that contained a binary brain. During the Clone Wars, he was a general of the highest order, but was gunned down by his own soldiers on the Banking Clan stronghold Mygeeto when Order 66 was enacted.

STASS ALLIE

- Homeworld: Coruscant
- Species: Human
- Gender: Female
- Height: 1.80 meters

During the Separatist crisis that threatened the Republic, Stass Allie advised the highest levels of the Republic's government. During the Clone Wars, Allie was made a member of the Jedi Council. After the fall of Saleucami in the Outer Rim Sieges, she was reassigned to the planet to lead mop-up operations with a contingent of clone troopers. When Order 66 was enacted, Allie was assassinated by her clone troopers while on a speeder bike patrol.

SAESEE TIIN

- Homeworld: Iktotch
- Species: Iktotchi
- Gender: Male
- Height: 1.88 meters

Saesee Tiin was always a bit of a loner. Though he served on the Jedi Council for years, he was never known to take a Padawan. Tiin was a devout believer of all Jedi teachings, almost to the point of fanaticism. Often misunderstood by his peers, his reputation as one of the Jedi order's best pilots and most skilled warriors was well earned. Tiin accompanied Jedi Master Mace Windu when he confronted Darth Sidious and was murdered by the Sith Lord.

AGEN KOLAR

- **Homeworld:** Iridonia
- **Species:** Zabrak
- **Gender:** Male
- **Height:** 1.90 meters

Agen Kolar was a warrior through and through. He was renowned for his lightsaber skills, not for his diplomacy. Kolar survived the battle on Geonosis, though his Padawan was killed. To Kolar's loyal mind, service to the Republic was the backbone of Jedi duty. He gladly became a general during the Clone Wars and was assigned to Brentaal IV, where he was overtaken and captured. Ultimately freed by Jedi Master Shaak Ti, Kolar returned to Coruscant, where he was killed by Darth Sidious.

KIT FISTO

- **Homeworld:** Glee Anselm
- **Species:** Nautolan
- **Gender:** Male
- **Height:** 1.96 meters

An amphibious Nautolan from the Sabilon region of the water planet Glee Anselm, Kit Fisto had head tentacles that contained highly sensitive olfactory receptors, allowing him to detect pheromonal expressions of emotion and other changes in body chemistry. He could live in or out of water and was a mighty warrior. Fisto was present at the battle on Geonosis and was slain by Darth Sidious while attempting to apprehend the Sith Lord with Mace Windu.

AAYLA SECURA

- **Homeworld:** Ryloth
- **Species:** Twi'lek
- **Gender:** Female
- **Height:** 1.72 meters

A Rutian Twi'lek born to an influential clan on Ryloth, Aayla Secura was apprenticed to Quinlan Vos at a young age and was raised as a Jedi. Vos was like a father to Secura. When Vos was corrupted by the dark side while deep undercover for the Jedi Council, Secura went into a deep depression. It was at this time that her relationship with Kit Fisto began to deepen, bordering on infatuation, an emotion forbidden by the Jedi Order. Perhaps if the two had not been Jedi, the relationship would have grown into something more. During the Clone Wars, Secura was assigned to the Commerce Guild stronghold of Felucia. As Secura and her clone troopers prepared to overtake the Guild's droid army, Order 66 was enacted. Secura was gunned down from behind.

PLO KOON

- **Homeworld:** Dorin
- **Species:** Kel Dor
- **Gender:** Male
- **Height:** 1.88 meters

A descendant of a long line of Jedi, Plo Koon fought beside Qui-Gon Jinn and served on the Jedi Council for many years. Due to his alien origin, Koon wore protective goggles and a face-concealing antiox mask whenever in oxygen-rich environments. As one of the most ferocious Jedi warriors, he served as a general in the Clone Wars and was shot down by a squadron of clone troopers while flying reconnaissance over Cato Neimoidia when Order 66 was enacted.

STAR WARS

Coming to the Cine-Manga® Galaxy!

CINE-MANGA®